Milo's Great Invention

Acknowledgments

Executive Editor	Stephanie Muller
Product Manager	Wendy Whitnah
Senior Supervising Editor	Carolyn Hall
Senior Design Manager	Pamela Heaney
Contributing Editor	Donna Rodgers
Electronic Production Artist	Bo McKinney
Program Author	Gare Thompson

Library of Congress Cataloging-in-Publication Data
Clements, Andrew, 1949–
   Milo's great invention / written by Andrew Clements ; illustrated by Barbara Johansen Newman.
      p.   cm.
   Summary: Milo, who does not share his family's fondness for peas, invents a machine to make the unpleasant vegetables disappear.
   ISBN 0-8172-5159-6
   [1. Inventions — Fiction.   2. Peas — Fiction.   3. Food habits — Fiction.]
I. Newman, Barbara Johansen, ill.   II. Title.
PZ7.C51198Mi   1998
[E] — dc21
                                                                97-25473
                                                                CIP   AC

1 2 3 4 5 6 7 8 9 F 01 00 99 98 97

Milo's Great Invention

Written by Andrew Clements
Illustrated by Barbara Johansen Newman

RSVP

RAINTREE
STECK-VAUGHN
PUBLISHERS
The Steck-Vaughn Company

Austin, Texas

Contents

Milo's Problem

Milo's mom and dad loved peas. Milo's big brother Ed loved peas. Milo's sister Anne loved peas. Well, their dog Snap didn't love peas. Milo did NOT love peas.

Milo tried to eat peas with butter and salt. He tried to eat peas without chewing. He tried to eat peas with grape jelly. No matter what he tried, Milo still did not love peas. He didn't even like them. He needed to find a way to get rid of peas.

Monday, September 25

Dear Journal,
We had peas at dinner again last night! I stared at them. They didn't go away. I hid them in my shirt pocket. Today Mom found my peas in the washing machine.
Now I have a better idea. I'll invent a machine to get rid of peas. I'll never have to eat peas again! I'll start on it tomorrow.

A Great Idea

Milo came home from school. He decided that he needed to learn more about peas. He put some frozen peas on his desk. Milo wrote down some facts about peas.

Peas are green. Peas are round. Round things can roll. "Aha!" Milo said to himself. "Peas can roll. That's it. I'll make peas roll in my invention!"

He tried rolling the peas down his shirt. He thought they would land in a bucket under his desk. But they got stuck on his clothes. He needed a better idea.

Tuesday, September 26
Dear Journal,
   We had peas again last night! I couldn't get the peas off my plate! I always sit by Dad and Anne at dinner. Dad sees everything. If Anne sees me do something, she'll tell on me. Maybe I could feed them to the dog. No, Snap won't eat peas.
   I could cut a hole in the table. No, that wouldn't work. Mom and Dad would be mad. If only I could think of a way to get rid of peas.

Inventor at Work

Milo needed some ideas to build his invention. He looked around the house. First, Milo found an old spoon in the kitchen. He also found a big roll of silver tape. In the basement, he found a long, thin hose. Peas could fit inside the hose.

In the garage, Milo saw a big vacuum cleaner. He looked at the long hose he had found. Then he looked at the big vacuum cleaner again. Milo got an idea.

Wednesday, September 27

Dear Journal,

At last, I know what my invention will be. It will have three parts. The first part will be the special spoon. The spoon will have a hole in it.

The second part will be the hose. The hose will hook onto the spoon.

The third part will be the big vacuum cleaner. The big vacuum cleaner can hook onto the hose. It will be a great invention! I'll call it

MILO'S
Peas-Be-Gone!

Pea

1. Spoon

Peas go down

2. Hose

BIG
VAC

Peas
in
here!

3. Vacuum

13

Putting It All Together

    Milo needed help to build his invention. He had to keep it a secret though. Milo asked his big brother Ed for help. "Can you make a hole in this spoon?" asked Milo.

    "Sure, but why do you want a hole in it?" asked Ed. He frowned at Milo.

    "Well, I'm going to make something disappear," said Milo. "But I need to keep it a secret."

15

Thursday, September 28

Dear Journal,

Well, I got Ed to help me. He made a hole in the spoon. Now the peas can fall from my spoon into the hose. It's perfect. Then the vacuum cleaner will suck them up! The peas will be gone.

It will look like I'm eating peas! I will cough so no one can hear the noise of the vacuum cleaner. I can't wait to try it. Tomorrow is the **BIG DAY!**

The Experiment

Milo raced home from school to try his invention. No one else was home. Milo heated some peas in the microwave oven. He put them on a dish.

Milo set up his invention. He sat down and picked up some peas with his spoon. The peas went down the hose. But they got stuck and came back out! There was no one to turn on the vacuum cleaner so the experiment didn't work. Milo had to solve this new problem.

Friday, September 29

Dear Journal,
My experiment didn't work! I have to get someone to turn on the vacuum cleaner. Then I can "eat" the peas. But who? I can't ask Ed or Anne. They might tell on me.

I know! I can ask Jenna, my friend who lives next door. She hates peas, too. We can set up a signal, and she can turn it on! This is a good plan!

Milo talked to Jenna. She said she would help. Jenna would turn on the vacuum cleaner just after Milo's mom sat down.

That night, Milo sat down at the dinner table. He looked out the window. Jenna waved. Mom put peas in front of him. He took a big helping. He put them on his spoon. Then Mom sat down.

Suddenly there was a huge noise. Then the peas disappeared from Milo's plate. It worked! Everyone stared at Milo.

Dad said, "What in the world is that?"

Milo said, "It's my invention called Milo's Peas-Be-Gone! It gets rid of peas."

"If you don't like peas, why didn't you just say so?" asked Mom. "I know another way you can try them. Put some peas in your mashed potatoes."

He tried it. He liked it! Milo decided to save his invention. He might need it if Mom ever served liver.